Dragon Kite of the Autumn Moon

THE ISLAND OF TAIWAN (often called Formosa from 1590, when the Portuguese landed there, until the time of the Second World War) lies 100 miles from the mainland of southern China. The custom of celebrating a special Kite's Day in the ninth month of the year, six days before the rising of the full moon, was probably taken to Taiwan by the Chinese, who began to settle there in the seventh century. Tradition holds that if the kites are set free at the end of the day, they will carry all troubles away with them. To avert inheriting the misfortune carried by the kites, they must be burned when they fall to earth.

TO MY MOM AND IN MEMORY OF MY DAD,
for all their encouragement over the years.
AND TO SUSAN AND JUDIT,
the editorial midwives who helped in the birth of this dragon.
Valerie Reddix

TO MY BELOVED MOTHER
Jean Tseng

With special thanks to Tom Casselman, Jim Miller, and Dave Gomberg, of the American Kitefliers Association, for their generous assistance; and with much appreciation to Michael Ma, at Hop Louie's, for taking time to answer all my questions; and to the reference librarians of the Anaheim and Los Angeles libraries, for their intrepid search for information.

Library of Congress Cataloging in Publication Data
Reddix, Valerie, Dragon kite of the autumn moon / Valerie Reddix ;
illustrated by Jean and Mou-sien Tseng.
p.   cm. Summary: When his grandfather is sick, Tad-Tin goes out to fly his special dragon kite, so that it can take all their troubles away with it. ISBN 0-688-11030-4. — ISBN 0-688-11031-2 (lib. bdg.) [1. Taiwan—Fiction.   2. Kites—Fiction.   3. Grandfathers—Fiction.]   I. Tseng, Jean ill.   II. Tseng, Mou-sien ill.   III. Title. PZ7.R2447Dr   1992
[E]—dc20   91-15066   CIP   AC

Dragon Kite
of the Autumn Moon

BY
VALERIE REDDIX

ILLUSTRATED BY
JEAN AND MOU-SIEN TSENG

LOTHROP, LEE & SHEPARD BOOKS   NEW YORK

It was the ninth day of the ninth month, and all over Formosa, kites had been flying since early morning. Every year, for as long as Tad-Tin could remember, Grandfather had made a special kite for Kite's Day.

As soon as it was ready, he and Tin would rush through the rice fields to the hillside. Grandfather would hold the kite and throw it up into the wind as Tin ran ahead with the string. All day they would fly their kite, long past sunset, until the night was thick with stars.

Then Grandfather would take his knife and cut the string and say, "Go now and carry all our misfortune away."

But this year Grandfather lay sick on his bed, the yellow bamboo box kite unfinished on the floor. This year there would be no Kite's Day for Tad-Tin.

In his own room, Tin sat on his bed. He stared at the dragon kite that hovered above him. Grandfather had made the dragon kite for Tin when he was born. Once a year, on his birthday, Tin would take the dragon kite down from the ceiling and fly it with Grandfather.

Of all the kites Grandfather had ever made, none could compare with the big dragon kite. A life lay hidden somewhere deep within its bamboo bones and red silk skin; a deep magic glowed behind its green lantern eyes. When the little harp in its mouth sang in the wind, the dragon almost seemed to be calling to Tin from the sky.

Every morning, the wild dragon's face welcomed Tin into a new day. And when Tin went to bed, its long bamboo body stretched over him, keeping him safe through the night.

Grandfather, too, had always been there, greeting him in the morning, hugging him good night.

Now the sun was low in the autumn sky. Kite's Day would soon be over. Tin crept into Grandfather's room and over to his bed. He leaned forward and whispered, "It's me, Grandfather."

Grandfather's eyes opened, dark and shining beneath his feathery eyebrows. "Such a small face to hold so big a frown," he said, his voice as dry as the rustle of rice paper. "I am sorry, my little grandson. Maybe next year we will have a kite to fly together."

Grandfather looked pale and weak. He was taking a long time to get better. If only the box kite were finished. Tin would fly it alone. He would cut the string himself. "Go now," he would say, "and carry all our misfortune away," and Grandfather would get well.

Then Tin remembered. He leaned closer to Grandfather. "I *have* a kite, Grandfather," he said. "Tonight, when the moon is high, I will fly the dragon kite."

"You wish to fly the dragon kite? It's much too heavy for you, Tin."

"I can do it."

"You know what will happen when you let it go and it comes back to earth."

Tin gazed out the window. "I know, Grandfather," he said. "It will be destroyed."

Grandfather lay quiet for a long time. At last he spoke. "I have taught you to believe in the old ways, as my grandfather taught me, as his grandfather did before him. You must go, Tin, and do what is in your heart to do."

Tin took a stool into his room and placed it on his bed. He climbed up and reached for the dragon kite. He freed its shiny red silk tail. He untied the cords that held its long, bony body. Then he unfastened the dragon's head.

For a long time he sat on his bed, holding the dragon kite in his arms. He cradled the dragon's face in his hands.

When Grandmother called Tin to supper, he picked his fish apart and poked at his rice.

Grandmother frowned. "You won't have the strength to fly your dragon if you don't eat," she said.

"I'm already full," Tin said, pushing his bowl away.

"Go on, then," she replied softly.

Tin took out the spool of twine. Carefully, he knotted it through the hook on the dragon's chest and pulled it tight. He shouldered the kite and stepped out into a night thick with stars.

The moon hung in the sky like a dragon's pearl. The night was filled with the scent of jasmine and, beneath it, a wild smell of sea and moonlight. The wind blew warm and strong—a good kite-wind.

Panting, Tin slowly climbed to the top of the hill. Only one window glowed in the house below, where Grandfather lay pale as a winter moon and Grandmother sat watching beside him. The dark shapes of a butterfly and, beyond it, a centipede drifted across the sky, their strings trailing behind them.

Tin stroked his dragon's knobby bamboo spine and ran his fingers along its soft, shimmering tail. For a long time he stood in the moonlight with the wind full in his face, chilling his tears.

Then he knelt, taking a box of matches from his pocket. He reached into the dark holes of the dragon's eyes and lit the lanterns. As he gazed into the light, he thought of his kite drifting above him, then crashing to the ground.

"I wish you could be free, little dragon," he said, "and never fall back to earth."

Tin stood up and held the dragon kite's head into the wind. He would have to run harder than he had ever run to launch the heavy kite by himself. It sighed and its tail rippled and snapped restlessly, as if it were eager to fly.

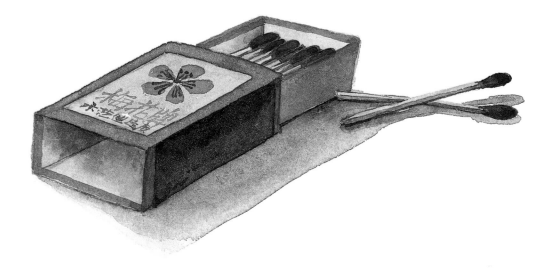

The wind surged about Tin. The time had come.

Tin took a deep breath and began to run. The wind roared in his ears. It lifted the kite's bamboo spine. Faster and faster he ran. The dragon seemed heavier and longer than ever. The wind whistled around the kite, jerking it out of Tin's hands.

The dragon dipped and darted like a wild thing, nearly pulling Tin off the ground. Tin's lungs ached. But still he ran, clutching the spool of twine. Suddenly the dragon kite began to climb.

Tin stopped. He held the twine tight against the dragon's tugging strength. The spool spun round and round in his hands as the dragon kite rose higher. Up and up it flew.

The dragon kite moaned, calling to Tin, dancing on the wind, weaving among the stars.

Never had Tin seen anything as lovely as this moon-washed dragon kite that Grandfather had made for him. He wondered whether Grandfather would ever make anything so lovely again.

Tin brushed a tear from his cheek and pulled out his pocket knife. Only the knot of the string was left on the spool.

"Goodbye, little dragon. I love you forever." He slashed the string.

"Go now," Tin whispered, "and take all our misfortune…"

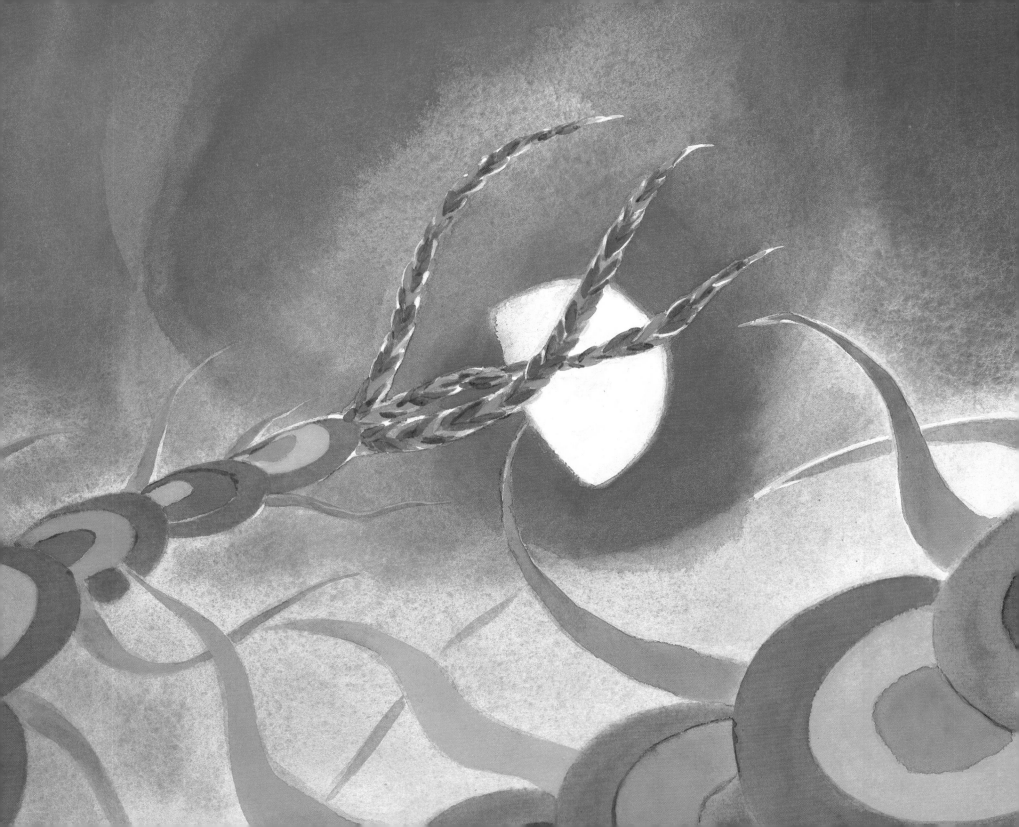

The moaning of the harp grew loud and wild. The long silk tail began to grow, beating hard against the wind. Tin gasped as the little bamboo discs burst like eggshells.

Suddenly a huge dragon was racing across the moon, twisting with joy. For a moment it hovered high above Tin. Then it dove toward the ground. Tin held his breath, his heart pounding.

The dragon swooped low, its jade-green eyes glinting at
Tin. From deep inside the dragon came a soft, rumbling
laugh, a kindly laugh. It circled the hill, then soared off over
the fields, away over the mountains.
Then the dragon was gone.

Tin ran down the hill to the house and up the steps to Grandfather's room.

Grandfather was sitting up in his bed, silver in the moonlight. When he saw Tin, his eyes sparkled and he opened his arms.

From somewhere deep inside Grandfather came a soft, rumbling laugh, a kindly laugh, and his arms closed around Tin.